THIS BOOK BELONGS TO

. . . .

. . . .

To Wren and Ivor, with love – T.K.

To Robin, with love – J.B.

First published 2021 by Macmillan Children's Books
an imprint of Pan Macmillan
The Smithson, 6 Briset Street, London EC1M 5NR
EU representative: Macmillan Publishers Ireland Limited,
Mallard Lodge, Lansdowne Village, Dublin 4
Associated companies throughout the world
www.panmacmillan.com

Hardback ISBN: 9781509848577
Paperback ISBN: 9781509848584

1 3 5 7 9 8 6 4 2

A CIP catalogue record for this book is available from the British Library.

Printed in China

SOMETIMES I AM
FURIOUS

TIMOTHY
KNAPMAN

JOE
BERGER

MACMILLAN CHILDREN'S BOOKS

Sometimes I'm a princess
who is thoughtful, brave and sweet.

Sometimes I'm the kindest fairy you could hope to meet.

And sometimes I am furious.

Sometimes I like digging.

Sometimes I make cakes.

Sometimes I don't mind it

when the grown-ups
make mistakes.

But **SOMETIMES**

I am furious.

Sometimes I play nicely.

Sometimes I can share.

Sometimes, though, I notice things that simply

ARE
NOT
FAIR!

SO SOMETIMES

With Mummy **AND** with Daddy too,
who **DARE** to tell me
what to do!

With naughty, **GREEDY** little boys,
who want to play with
all my toys!

They make me **CRY**

AND

SCR

AND

I don't want **THIS!**
It's just **NO GOOD!**

It won't do
things I think
it **SHOULD!**

It's **MUCH** too big!

It's **FAR** too small!

It **WILL NOT**, **WILL NOT** work at all!

It's **VERY, VERY, VERY BAD!**

SO

SOMETIMES

SOMETIMES

I AM FU

RIOUS!

But afterwards
I'm sad.

I'm all alone.
I'm in a muddle.
I'm wet with tears.
I need a cuddle.

Then someone puts me on her knee
and knows that I don't mean to be
so furious. She says, "Poor you!
When you get cross, here's what to do . . ."

And then she whispers in my ear
everything I need to hear,
and all the bad things disappear.

So now I can play nicely.
Look at me, I share.

And even when I notice things
that simply **ARE NOT FAIR** . . .

I take deep breaths.

I count to ten.

I sing my happy song.

And now
when I am

It's not for very long.